trying to cheat back, so I declare that Eric the ferret, who was last, shall be first, and that Girarfa, who was first, shall be last. Because if I'm going to hand over as mayor for the day, it certainly won't be to someone I can't trust.'

Eric still remembers what a happy day he spent as mayor. And Girarfa still hasn't forgotten that painful lesson he learned, how the first can end up last, and the last first.

Heavenly Father, help us never to do wrong so that people will admire us. Help us to be people whom others can trust.

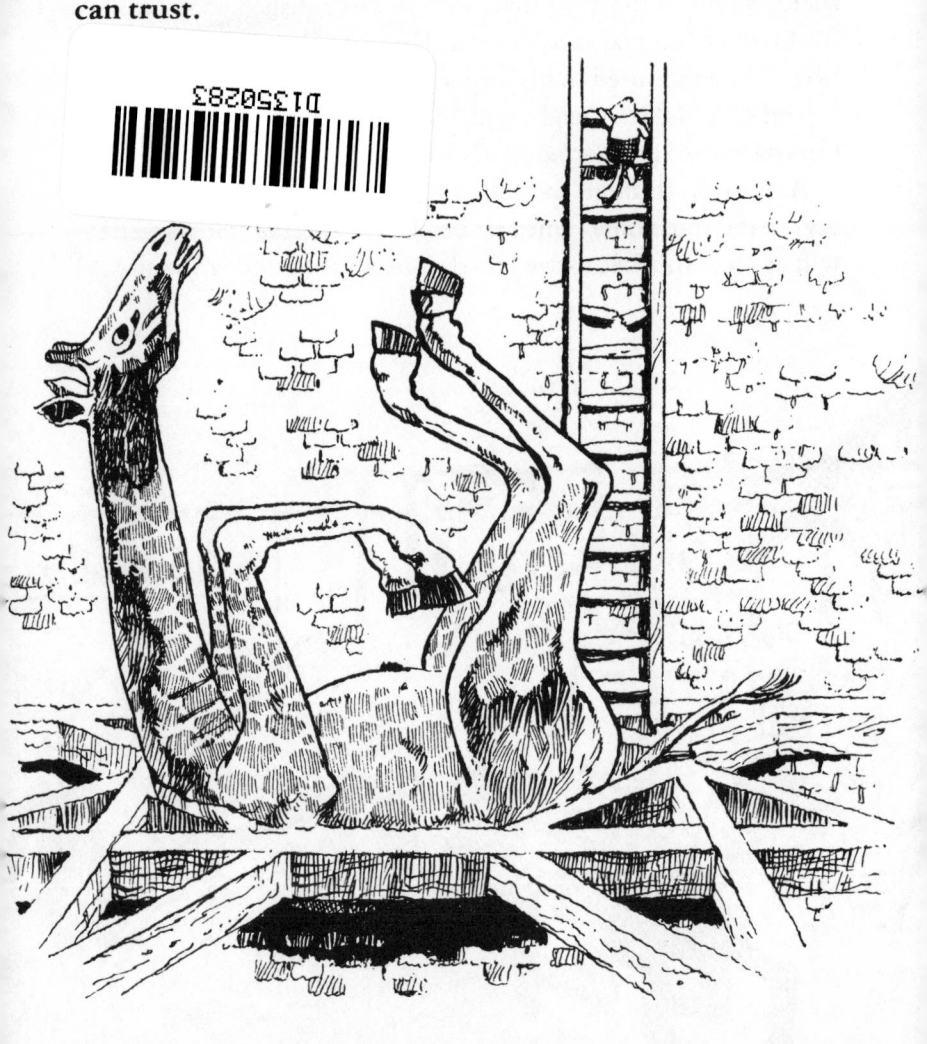

you. If you rescue me, I promise I'll race properly.' So Eric the ferret stopped, lowered his tail and pulled Girarfa up.

They didn't stop to speak, but slid down the ladders as fast as they could. Eric shot off, but came to a sudden and agonising stop when he found that the giraffe had tied his tail to the bottom of the ladder. 'Sorry you're too tied up to join me,' Girarfa cackled as he bolted on ahead to finish the marathon first. Eric felt like giving up, but slowly he untied his tail and jogged along to the school to complete the race.

Next day was the prizegiving, and all the quadrupeds were there. Right in the front row, with newly-polished hoofs and freshly-combed ears, was Girarfa. Up stood the mayor. 'First prize,' he announced in his important mayor's voice, 'in the Grand Old Maiden Quadrupeds' Marathon Race goes,' and here Girarfa smiled an enormous, toothy smile, 'to Eric the ferret.'

A gasp ran through the hall. The mayor went on, 'The referee says that Girarfa only came first because he cheated. He wanted to win at all costs. Eric carried on despite all this, and without

IGNATIUS GOES FISHING
and More Beastly Tales

© Text Philip Welsh 1984

© Illustrations Scripture Union 1984

First published 1984
Fourth reprint 1989

ISBN 0 86201 207 4

The stories *Hercules the Secret Service Flea* and *It's Not Much Fun Being a Slug* first
appeared in the magazine *Together* published by the Church of England Board of
Education.

By the same author: **The Reluctant Mole and Other Beastly Tales**

Printed and bound in Great Britain by Ebenezer Baylis & Son Ltd,
The Trinity Press, Worcester, and London.

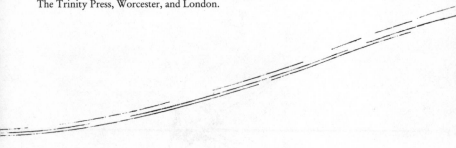

IGNATIUS GOES FISHING

and More Beastly Tales

by Philip Welsh

Illustrated by Fred Apps

SCRIPTURE UNION
130 City Road, London EC1V 2NJ

Dedicated
to my godchildren,
Ellen, Edward, Andrew, James
and Philip.

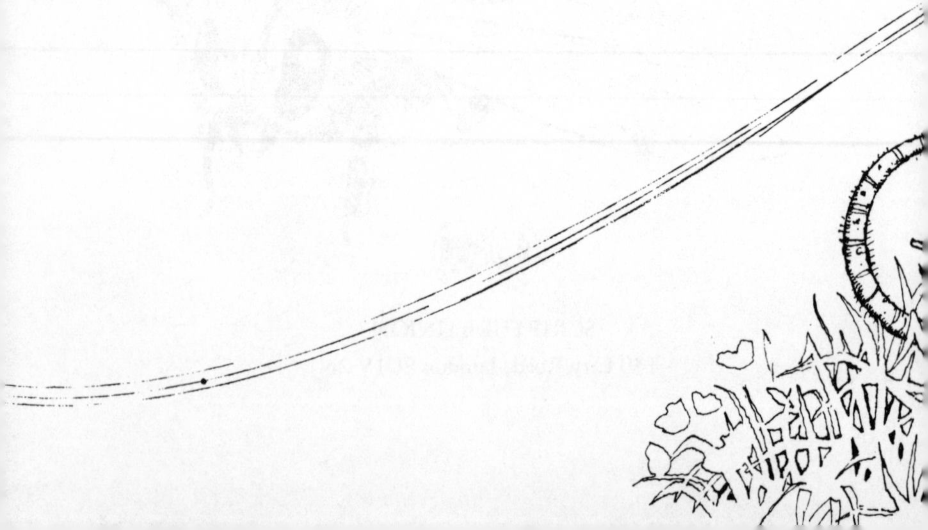

Dear Reader,

Every now and then I've been getting letters from complete strangers, telling me how they've enjoyed the stories in 'The Reluctant Mole', and demanding to know when I'll be bringing out another book.

Well, here it is, once again with splendidly seedy pictures by Fred Apps, and with thanks to all those kind people who kept asking for more.

Old friends are here, like Ignatius the Church Mouse, Archie the Performing Flea, Harold the Mole and Arfa the Disgusting Camel. Even Major Feele-Gloomy makes a brief and disastrous appearance. Since last time I've moved to a new church, but to my surprise all the animals have come with me, and have made new friends whom you'll discover in the following pages.

Anyway, my typewriter is feeling battered and weary, and both my typing fingers are an inch shorter than they used to be, so it's time I stopped nattering and left you to enjoy the stories.

Philip Welsh

Contents

Most people don't know that our church mouse, Ignatius, is
mad about fishing. Every Saturday, when he's finished
sweeping the leaves out of the church porch, he gets his
fishing rod out of its hiding place up the tower, puts on his
wellingtons and an old fishing hat, and goes down to the river.
There he sits all day, staring at the water, and often doesn't come
home till the football comes on television.

One Saturday when he was there, sitting absolutely still on the
bank, with ten packets of crisps still unopened at his side, all of a
rush up galloped Arfa the camel.

'Oh Ignatius,' he said, as he clattered to a standstill, 'I don't
know what to do. The Council's offered me a new house, but it's
miles away, and I've got to go and see it this afternoon. Can you
come with me? I need some help.'

''Fraid not, old man,' said the mouse. 'Any other time I'd love
to come, but I'm in the middle of fishing now.' So Arfa went
away.

Later that afternoon, when there were only five packets of crisps
left, Ignatius suddenly saw a peculiar shape in the water coming
towards him. 'My goodness,' he thought, 'It must be the cassock
'n' onion flavouring in the crisps, going to my head.'

To his amazement, out of the river came his old friend Harvey

the Octopus. 'Oh Ignatius,' said Harvey as he dripped all over the crisps, 'I'm so glad I've caught you. My mum's tied herself in a knot and I don't know what to do. Can you come and help?'

'What a pity,' said the mouse. 'Any other time I'd be round like a shot. But right now I'm busy fishing.' So Harvey went away.

As the sun was going down, and Ignatius had just one soggy bag of curry 'n' woodworm crisps left, there came through the gloom a long, pointed, furry nose, and just behind it Harold the Mole. 'I thought I'd find you here,' he said. 'I'm feeling a bit fed up tonight on my own, so I thought I'd see if you fancied some cocoa and a couple of juicy antburgers.'

'Oh dear,' said the mouse, 'it'll have to be another night, I'm afraid. As soon as I've finished fishing I've got to get back and see the big match.' So Harold went away.

When it got to ten to ten, Ignatius packed up his fishing rods and ran back to see the match. He hadn't caught a single fish. Served him right.

Next morning, Ignatius was patrolling as usual underneath the bench where the choirboys sat, trying to decide which ankle to bite first. Suddenly he heard the magic word 'fishing'. He stopped and listened, and it was a story about two brothers who went fishing one day. When they were in the middle of their fishing, up came Jesus and said to them, 'Can you come with me? I need your help.' And straight away they dropped everything and went with him.

Ignatius felt dreadful. He remembered the day before, and how his three friends had asked him to help them, but he'd just carried on fishing. So the following Saturday he made an astounding decision. He decided not to go fishing, but instead to go and see the people he'd let down the week before. He'd remember now to help people when they asked for help, not when he felt like it.

Heavenly Father, make us ready to help other people, not just when we feel like it, but when they ask for our help.

THE REVENGE OF JASPER THE TOAD

Opposite the church there were two small houses with two very different gardens. The first garden was full of long grass, and in the grass lived a rather elegant fellow called Godfrey the Grasshopper, who liked nothing better than to sway about on top of a tall piece of grass, chirping, as grasshoppers do.

The second garden was full of mud, and in the middle of the mud there lay a large and dirty pond. This was the home of Jasper the Toad, and he liked nothing better than to flop around in the mud all day, croaking so loudly it made the pond shiver.

The odd thing was, though Godfrey and Jasper couldn't have been more different, they were the best of friends, because they'd always lived next door to each other and had grown up together. Every Sunday afternoon they'd have a race to see who could hop to the church and back faster. Whoever lost had to listen to the other one singing.

But as they got older, bit by bit they saw less of each other. Godfrey was very clever. He passed all his exams at school and got a job in an office, hopping off to the train every morning looking very important.

Jasper was no good at exams. He was always bottom of the class. But he was brilliant at fixing things. Every Saturday morning you'd see his bony toad's legs sticking out from under somebody's car, that he was fixing for them. In the end he got a job at the local garage as a mechanic, and you could always find him by looking for a car that was croaking.

By this time, sad to say, Godfrey and Jasper hardly saw each other at all. Then one day, Godfrey was hopping his elegant way home from the station, with his shiny briefcase on one arm, his neatly rolled umbrella on the other arm and a tiny bowler hat on his head, not looking where he was going. Just ahead of him, lying as usual under a car engine, was Jasper, with his lanky toad's legs stretching right across the pavement.

With a horrible shriek, Godfrey tripped over the legs and went flying. His briefcase burst open, and papers from work went all over the road.

'You idiot toad, Jasper,' he hissed, mad with rage. 'If you didn't waste your time messing about with stupid cars, you wouldn't get in the way of people like me.'

Jasper wasn't going to take this lying down. 'Just who do you think you are, Godfrey?' he shouted back, waving an oily fist at the grasshopper. 'Why don't you do a real day's work for once, and get your hands dirty, instead of fiddling about with bits of paper in a boring old office?'

They both went off angrily into their gardens, and from that day on they didn't speak a word to each other.

Months later, when Godfrey arrived at work one morning, there on his desk was a letter from head office. 'We want to give you a better job,' it said. 'Come to head office at once. A car will be waiting for you downstairs.'

Full of excitement, Godfrey rushed down and found a huge, sleek car, complete with chauffeur. Off he went, feeling *very* pleased with himself.

When they were half way there, the car broke down with a sickening crunch. 'Oh no,' said Godfrey, 'I'll never get the new job if I don't get there on time.'

'Don't worry,' said the driver. 'There's a garage round the corner. I'll nip off and fetch someone.'

What should Godfrey hear, a few minutes later, but the familiar sound of a toad croaking a funny little tune. Coming round the corner just after the croak, Jasper arrived.

They stared at each other. 'Who was it said that fixing cars was stupid, eh, and a waste of time?' said Jasper. 'If I'm so dim, why doesn't a clever chap like you fix it yourself?'

'I'm sorry, Jasper,' said the grasshopper. 'I've been stupid myself. I thought I was clever, but I wasn't clever enough to see that people like you, who can fix things, are just as important as people like me, who can do paperwork.'

So Jasper got to work fixing the car. 'You know,' he said, with his head somewhere inside the engine, clanking away with his spanners, 'I could never see the point of the kind of job you do, in an office, but I've been wrong too. Now my garage work has grown, I've got all sorts of paperwork to do with the business. I could do with a bit of advice.'

'Righto,' said Godfrey. 'I'm glad we're friends again.'

'So am I,' said the toad. 'Tell you what, let's celebrate your new job on Sunday afternoon with one of our old hopping races.'

Heavenly Father, help us never to look down on people who have different gifts from us, but to learn to value them.

HERCULES THE SECRET SERVICE FLEA

No one had ever seen a flea with a better suntan than Hercules. He got it when he went on secret missions to far-away countries – because Hercules was a Secret Service flea. It seemed to run in his family; he was always saying how his great-great-great-grandfather was one of the Flea Musketeers.

Once when he was back home, staying with his brother Archie, he hopped along one day to the school fête, though nobody knew. But all the time he was there, he used his Secret Service cunning to help them make money for the school. This is how he did it. Every time it looked as if the customers were good shots, then just as they went to throw, Hercules would give them a flea-bite, which made them jump, so they missed and lost their money, which meant all the more money for the school!

Now Hercules was back again and this time his cunning came in even more useful. His brother Archie used to work in a flea circus. One day, while Hercules was having a bit of a lie-in, in rushed his brother and shook him till he woke up.

'Whassup?' groaned Hercules, still half asleep.

'It's no good,' said Archie. 'I can't go to the circus and do my tightrope act today. I'm sure I'm going to fall off.'

'Don't be soppy,' said Hercules. 'You've been walking that

tightrope for years and you haven't once fallen off. What's up with you?'

'I feel all panicky today,' said Archie. 'I just can't face it. It's like the feeling you get if you've got to take an exam or a test, or if you've got to go on stage.'

'I'll tell you what I'll do,' said Hercules, with his cunning little flea brain ticking away. 'I'll hide up in the circus roof, and we'll tie a piece of string round you, so thin that the audience can't see it. Then if you start to wobble, I'll pull the string to get you straight again.'

Archie felt much better. He knew he couldn't go wrong now.

When the time came, the show was terrific, and Archie did his act better than ever. As soon as he'd finished, he rushed out to see his brother. 'You were marvellous, Hercules,' he said. 'That rope you held me up with was so thin I couldn't even see it myself.'

'I'm not surprised,' his brother replied. 'There wasn't any rope. You did it by yourself. I played a trick on you.'

'Why, you treacherous old Secret Service flea!' Archie cried. 'I could have killed myself.'

'Oh no you couldn't,' said Hercules. 'I knew you could do it, if you just stopped panicking. Everybody gets panicky once in a while; it's natural. But you've shown yourself now that you don't

need any secret rope to hold you up, and I bet you won't panic so easily again.'

Archie felt much happier after that, and went off cheerfully to work each day. As for Hercules, he just disappeared one morning. It must have been another Secret Service mission.

Heavenly Father, help us not to panic if we have to do something new. Help us not to be frightened of making a mistake.

IGNATIUS HAS A DREAM

Early one Sunday morning Ignatius woke up, stretched and said to himself, 'Today I think I'll go to the service, and see what they get up to in church.' First he had a quick bite to eat. For the last few days he'd been chewing his way through an old story-book he had come across. He called it his breakfast serial.

Then he wriggled into his special mouse's four-legged pinstriped church trousers, and crept into church just in time to squeeze himself in between a very fat Cub and a very thin Brownie, so no one could see him.

He could hardly breathe with all the people there. And what with being squashed, and singing as loudly as he could, and having eaten one too many chapters for breakfast, he began to feel very peculiar. So he staggered out of the church, and tottered around the churchyard, unable to make his legs go straight.

All of a sudden a great, grey gravestone loomed up in front of him. As it came closer and closer he started to read the old writing on it: 'Sacred to the memory of Elizabeth Try, for thirty years schoolmistress of this parish, died eighteen –'

'Wham!' With a great crunching of nose, Ignatius walked right into the gravestone, and knocked himself out.

20

As he lay there, with his four legs, in his four-legged pinstriped church trousers, pointing to the sky, Ignatius had a dream. He dreamt he was in the old school. And there, at the far end of the old school hall, in an old-fashioned dress, sat Miss Elizabeth Try. The whole class – about fifty of them – sat in front of her on wooden benches, silently, because they could see the cane hanging on the wall behind her.

As Ignatius looked at her from the back of the hall, through the gaslight and the smoke from the coal fire, he heard her telling the story of Jesus when he went to the Temple and found that it was more like a market. He'd thrown their tables to the ground and said, 'My house shall be a house of prayer, not a robber's cave.'

'Now where have I heard that before?' thought Ignatius. 'I know, it was in church this morning, just before I started feeling funny . . .'

Then everything started going fuzzy and fading away, and suddenly he found himself back in the present again, lying on the grass in the churchyard. 'I must have walked right into that gravestone,' he groaned as he rubbed his sore nose, which had got bent sideways when he hit the stone. 'Oh well,' he pondered, as he crept back into the church, 'at least I'll be able to smell round corners now.' And that's just what he did.

As he went through the door, he was sure he could smell somebody's lunch. There, at the back of the church, was his friend Oliver the bat, who usually lived up the tower. In each of his leathery wings he had a packet of crisps, special bat crisps. One was cheese and ants flavour, the other was pigeons and vinegar. Oliver was munching and crunching as fast as he could.

'What do you think you're up to,' said Ignatius, 'sitting and eating your lunch here in church?'

'Why shouldn't I?' said the bat. 'It's cold up in that tower.'

Then Ignatius remembered his dream, and the story he'd heard Miss Try tell. 'I'll tell you why,' he said. 'It's because this isn't just any old building, it's what Jesus called a house of prayer. That means it's a special place for worshipping God and for saying your prayers, and for being quiet and thinking. Not for running around or chattering or eating your lunch.'

'Can't you say your prayers anywhere?' the bat muttered through the crumbs.

'Of course you can,' said Ignatius, 'But a church is a special place to help us think of God, and that's not so easy if there's a fat bat in the back seat deafening you with his lunch.'

'You know, mouse,' said the bat, 'you're a bit pompous sometimes, but you're right. What do you want me to do with my crisps, then?'

Ignatius was beginning to feel a bit peckish by now, so he said, 'Let's go outside and think about it. Maybe I can give you a hand.'

Heavenly Father, thank you for the churches where we worship you. Help us to remember that they are special places to remind us of you.

SUPERFROG

Down in the boiler room underneath the church, there used to live a frog called Sydney. Sydney's job was to check that the Vicar remembered to turn the boiler on to heat the church on Sundays. If he forgot, Sydney would hop through the Vicarage letter-box and flop on to the doormat, croaking away till the Vicar remembered.

One day Sydney was bored, so he hopped on a bus and went to see the new Superman film. He thought it would be terrific to be like that – one minute leading an ordinary life, the next minute able to do anything you like. 'That's what I'll be,' he said. 'I'm fed up with being boring old Sydney from the boiler room. From now on they can call me Superfrog!'

All the way home on the bus he puffed out his spotty green chest, looked the other passengers dead in the eye and croaked under his breath, 'Superfrog – I can do anything!'

When he got home to his boiler room, still croaking the magic word, 'Superfrog!', Sydney sat down and had a think. 'What shall I do, then? I know – I'll join the choir.'

So he went along to the choir practice that afternoon, really pleased with himself. At last he'd had the nerve to try something new. So they tested him. 'Sing this note,' said the choirmaster, and out came a great croak. 'Try this one instead.' Out came a huge honk. 'It's a froghorn,' said one of the choirboys.

Sydney tried and tried and tried, but it was no good.

As he flopped slowly down the steps to his boiler room, Sydney felt so ashamed. 'I'm no good,' he said. 'I'm useless,' as a great tear dribbled down his fat, froggy face.

Just at that moment, who should be going past the door but Ignatius, the church mouse, doing his rounds to check that the church was all right. When he heard the dismal dripping noise from Sydney's room, he tapped on the door and said, 'What's up, Sydney? Are you all right?'

'I was bored,' said Sydney as he opened the door, 'so I thought I'd try something new, and join the choir. But I was useless. I'm no good at anything.'

'Don't be daft,' said the mouse, 'just because you've been disappointed once. Everyone's good at something. Remember Harvey the octopus? He thought it was the end of the world when they wouldn't let him take up ballet dancing – until I told him to take up wrestling instead. What about you?'

'All I can do is hop,' said the frog, 'Hop and honk. What good's that? I –' Suddenly Sydney stopped talking. He'd caught sight of someone creeping out of the church, with what looked like the choir's silver trophy stuck up his jumper. Quick as a flash, with a mighty hop Sydney leaped down the burglar's neck and landed – inside the silver cup.

'Clang!' went the lid as the burglar slammed it down on top of the frog and ran off. What could Sydney do? He was trapped. He took a deep breath, inflated his spotty green chest as far as it would stretch, and let out a stupendous froghorn croak.

The burglar was terrified to find himself running along with his own burglar alarm. So he threw the trophy down, with Sydney still honking away inside, and ran away as fast as he could and was never seen again.

'Thank goodness,' said the choirmaster to Sydney that evening, 'that you can jump better than anyone else. And thank goodness you've got a voice like a froghorn after all. To show you how grateful we are, we're going to make you an honorary member of the choir. You can sit with us in church every Sunday, with a ruff round your neck and an enormous pile of music books – only don't try to sing.'

Sydney was overjoyed, and every single Sunday he's there, singing away silently. Though sometimes, as they listen to the choir, the people suspect that the odd frog-note slips out.

Heavenly Father, thank you for giving each of us different things to be good at. Help us, if we try the wrong thing first, not to give up.

NAPOLEON THE ENVIOUS EARWIG

In a cardboard box in the church porch lived an earwig called Napoleon. It was a very superior box, but Napoleon was miserable. Normally he'd jump out of his box as soon as the sun came up, scamper down to the station, wiggle into someone's ear and go up to London for the day. But now he hadn't been out for ages. The other animals noticed that Napoleon had lost his wiggle, and began to get worried.

After they hadn't seen Napoleon for a week, they sent round his particular friend, Archie the performing flea. He found Napoleon sitting on his cardboard box looking dreadful. 'What's wrong?' said Archie.

'I'm fed up,' Napoleon replied, 'fed up with being a scruffy earwig. Why can't I be something glamorous like a butterfly, or something clever like a bee? I wouldn't even mind being a flea like you. I just wish I wasn't an ordinary earwig.'

'Well,' said Archie, trying to be helpful, 'it's amazing what they can do these days. Why don't you go and see two or three of the other insects, and see what they think?'

'Okay, I'll give it a try,' said Napoleon, and scuttled off.

First he went to the bottom of the churchyard, looking for Walter the Worm. 'I'm thinking of becoming a worm,' said the earwig. 'Then I could worm away under the earth all day, safe and snug and out of the rain.'

'I shouldn't bother if I were you,' said Walter. 'You never see a

29

soul, it's perishing cold down there, and if you're not careful someone sticks a fork through you. I always thought you were such a good earwig. It would be a shame for you to change.'

'I wonder,' thought Napoleon, and left.

Next he went down to the river to call on Neville the Newt. 'Well, this is an honour,' said the newt. 'What brings you here?'

'I'm fed up with being an earwig,' said Napoleon. 'I've always fancied being a newt, swimming around in the river all day instead of having to wiggle into people's dirty ears.'

'That's odd,' said Neville. 'I've often wished I could be an earwig. It's not much fun in the water, you know, day after day, trying to avoid the motor-boats and fishing lines and the great eels that want to swallow you up.'

Napoleon was surprised that Neville wanted to be like him. It cheered him up quite a lot. All the same, he thought he'd go and see one more friend, Plato the Centipede. He found Plato dozing peacefully in front of his fire, with his hundred feet nice and warm inside a hundred furry slippers.

'My goodness,' said Plato with a jump, 'It's you, Napoleon. I was just dreaming I was an earwig. It was such a nice dream. But what can I do for you?'

'I've come to ask your advice,' said Napoleon, 'About becoming a centipede.

If I had a hundred legs like you, just think how I could dance! Or imagine playing football with a hundred legs, they'd never be able to tackle me!'

Plato lost his temper. 'For goodness' sake, Napoleon, you daft earwig, why are you wasting all your time wishing you were someone else? That's called envy, and it stops you enjoying being the person you are.'

That made Napoleon think. He remembered how Walter admired him, and how Neville the Newt had wished he was an earwig. Even old Plato dreamed about it. Maybe it wasn't so bad after all.

'There's one other thing,' said Plato. 'Unless insects like us learn not to be envious of other animals, we'll end up no better than anyone else. They're always wishing they were clever like so-and-so, or good-looking like so-and-so, or rich like so-and-so.'

As Plato was saying this, Napoleon felt a strange sensation coming over him. Sure enough, his wiggle was coming back. 'No time to lose!' he shouted as he rushed out of Plato's house and down to the station to catch a passing ear. Now he'd stopped wishing he was everyone else instead of the person he was, he'd begun to enjoy life again.

Heavenly Father, you have made each one of us special. Help us not to envy other people, but to enjoy being the person you have made us.

THE WELLIGATOR

Just as it was getting dark one winter's afternoon, and the churchyard was silent and full of fog, Ignatius the church mouse decided to pop out of his nice warm room at the church to fetch some snow. He had been getting his tea ready, and fancied a snow sandwich. After his snow sandwich he was looking forward to his favourite tea-time treat, toasted hymnbooks, or as he called them, hymnburgers.

So out he went, into the fog and the snow. Suddenly, through the gloom, he saw a huge black shape coming towards him out of the fog. He turned to run back indoors, but with a crash the door slammed before he could get there. He was alone in the churchyard with the huge black shape, and it was getting nearer.

'Ignatius,' came a deep voice from the black shape. 'Ignatius,' it repeated, getting closer and closer.

Ignatius was so frightened he couldn't move a step. 'Who – who are you?' he said in a dry little whisper. And the great black shape replied, 'I am the terrible man-eating boot of Old Malden. In ancient times they called me the Welligator, and I have come for you, Ignatius. Follow me.'

Ignatius was frozen to the spot with fear, motionless except for a tiny icicle that trembled on the end of his nose. 'Come with me,' said the Welligator again, 'or else you will suffer welligation.'

Ignatius had no idea what welligation was, but it sounded awful, so he forced himself to follow the Welligator, through the fog and the snow and in between the gravestones, into the furthest and gloomiest corner of the churchyard.

The Welligator looked down at Ignatius, who shivered and whimpered. 'What were you doing, Ignatius, yesterday at four o'clock?'

'I was . . . I was having my tea,' said the church mouse, 'Yes, I was just making a nice trifle out of bits of old candles.'

'Don't you *trifle* with me,' boomed the boot. 'Tell me again, what were you doing?'

'I was with Archie,' Ignatius confessed in a tiny voice, 'Archie the flea.'

'And what were you doing with Archie the flea?' said the Welligator.

'We were playing snowballs,' said the mouse.

'I know you were playing snowballs,' said the hollow voice. 'And who was inside the snowball?'

'Archie,' murmured Ignatius.

'And do you know how I know?' the man-eating boot went on. 'Because the snowball rolled into my sitting-room, and when it melted in front of the fire, there was poor Archie the flea, frozen and soaked to the skin and frightened and very, very miserable.'

'I didn't think,' said Ignatius. 'I never meant to hurt him. It was all a game, see.'

'It was a good game for you,' said the Welligator. 'But you didn't bother to think about Archie, did you? You were enjoying yourself, so you didn't notice he was scared to death. You're not a bad mouse, Ignatius, but you just don't think about other people's feelings. That's why I'm going to welligate you.'

The man-eating boot got up on top of the tallest gravestone, ready to welligate Ignatius. The mouse was so scared he couldn't move. Then things went dreadfully wrong for the Welligator. He slipped on some ice and fell off the gravestone, and out from inside the great long boot there rolled one of Ignatius' best friends, Harold the Mole.

Ignatius was thunderstruck. He didn't know whether to be glad that he wasn't going to be welligated after all, or angry with Harold for playing this trick on him. 'Why did you do this to me?' he shouted at the mole.

'It was to teach you a lesson, Ignatius,' the mole replied. 'Archie was so upset yesterday, that I decided to give you a scare, so that you knew what it felt like yourself.'

'I suppose you're right,' grumbled Ignatius. 'It seemed a good game at the time, but it was a bit cruel. Do you want some tea, Harold? I've just remembered that I came out here to get some snow for a snow sandwich.'

'I've got a better idea,' said the mole. 'Let's go round and have tea with Archie, and cheer him up.'

'Good idea,' said the mouse. 'Then I can tell him I'm sorry. And just in case he only gives us a tiny flea tea, I'll take some of my hymnburgers.'

Heavenly Father, help us to remember other people's feelings, and never to be cruel to those weaker than ourselves.

SACRED
TO THE MEMORY
WILLIAM H.
BLOGGS
DIED 1870

REST IN
PEACE

IT'S NOT MUCH FUN BEING A SLUG

SLUG NOOK
HAWKERS -
TINKERS - TAXMEN -
ANYONE WELCOME

Usually the grass in the churchyard is so long and jungly that nobody would notice a large flat stone in one corner. But it's not just a stone, it's somebody's home. Underneath it lives Solomon the Slug, and he calls his home Slug Nook.

He lives there because slugs like to stay where it's dark and damp. That's why you often find them when you turn over flat stones. The trouble is, nobody likes slugs. Not that there's anything wrong with being a slug. It's just that they're peculiar creatures, and every time somebody's doing the garden, and they turn over a flat stone and find a clammy slug underneath, they go 'Oooergh!' and drop it as fast as they can. It's not much fun being a slug.

This used to happen to poor old Solomon every time people came to do the churchyard which, luckily for him, wasn't as often as they should. At first Solomon would think, 'Oh good, here comes somebody. I don't get many visitors.' But as soon as they spotted him they would go 'Oooergh!' and drop him to the ground.

Solomon began to despair. 'I know I'm not much to look at,' he said to himself. 'But if only they'd bother to get to know me a bit, they'd find out I'm not half as bad as they think. Maybe I should

37

just pack up my luggage' (or as he called it, 'my sluggage') 'and move away.' But he knew it would be just the same wherever he went.

Then one day, when he peeped out from underneath his flat stone, he noticed that there was a new gardener, an old chap called Len. Slowly Len weeded his way around the churchyard, until eventually he got to Solomon's gloomy corner, Slug Nook. Solomon knew what was coming. He gritted his teeth and shut his beady eyes as tight as he could, and waited for the worst.

Nothing happened. Slowly he opened first one beady eye, then the other, and gradually ungritted his teeth. There was Len the gardener, grinning down at him and chuckling, 'My goodness, I haven't seen such a great fat slug as you for ages.'

'What a cheek!' thought Solomon, though really he was pleased that someone was talking to him. They got chatting, and Solomon found himself saying all sorts of interesting things he didn't know he had in him, because nobody had ever bothered to listen before.

'But tell me,' he asked Len, 'why didn't you go 'Oooergh!' like everyone else, and shudder, and drop me to the ground?'

'Ah well, you see,' said the gardener, 'a few years ago, while I was weeding, I strained my back and had to go to hospital for a long time. The trouble was there was no room for me in the ordinary wards, so I had to go into the special Slug Unit. I was mad about this at the time, when I thought of all those horrible slugs I'd always heard about. But as I lay there day after day, with no one to talk to except the slugs, I found they weren't half as bad as I thought. The more I got to know them, the more I liked them. It's like some people. If you've never met anyone like them before, they give you the creeps, until you get to know them properly. Then you realise how daft you've been, and what you've been missing.'

Now, whenever Solomon hears the gardener coming, instead of gritting his teeth and clenching his beady eyes, he pokes his head out from under the stone to say hello. And Len comes along to do the churchyard more often then he used to, because he likes to see his sluggy little friend. But they'd never have been able to enjoy this if Len hadn't discovered that clammy slugs, like strange people, aren't half as bad as they seem, once you bother to get to know them.

Heavenly Father, forgive us when we shy away from people who are different from us. Help us to take the trouble to get to know them better.

SHERLOCK TO THE RESCUE

When the afternoons get darker and the ground gets frosty, Ignatius the church mouse gets very lazy. He curls up underneath the radiator in the vestry, and passes the day snoozing and toasting hymnbooks, to eat for his tea with shredded cassocks.

One afternoon he was busily looking for old books in the bottom of a cupboard, when he came across three old scraps of paper. 'That's handy,' he thought, 'an instant meal.' He picked up the nearest bit of old page, but just as he was about to pop it into his mouth, he saw something written on it. Ignatius wasn't a very good reader, so slowly he spelt out the two words. When he did, he froze to the spot.

In a frightened whisper he said, 'How did this bit of paper know I was going to eat it? Is this some sort of uncanny message?' There on the torn piece of paper he was about to chew up were the two mysterious words, 'inwardly digest'.

He snatched up the second scrap of paper. This had just one word on it. He could just make it out in the twilight. It simply said, 'embrace'.

Ignatius, who was a modest sort of mouse, blushed secretly under his fur. 'What sort of book is this?' he wondered. So he

40

looked for another clue. He picked up the third piece of torn page. This one said, 'hold fast'. 'Peculiar,' he thought. 'First this looked like bits of a book on digesting, then on embracing. Now it looks like a book on wrestling. This is a bit too much for me. I need a detective . . .' So he sent for his cousin, a weasel called Sherlock.

When Sherlock arrived at last, Ignatius explained his three pieces of torn paper. 'Fascinating, my dear mouse,' said the detective as he puffed away at his detective's curly pipe. 'Let's take a closer look. We may find another clue.'

Sure enough, down a crack between the floorboards in the cupboard, he could just make out some more scraps of paper. So he fished into the enormous pocket of his enormous detective's overcoat, and pulled out a long pair of tweezers. With these tweezers he picked out – or as detectives say, extricated – four more bits of the page. On each of them there seemed to be another word. The first said HEARTH. The second EMTORE. The third ADMARKLE.

'What's an admarkle?' said the mouse. 'This is worse than ever.' Then up came the fourth scrap, which said ARNAND.

For a long time Sherlock was silent, just puffing his curly pipe in a weasely way, and shuffling the bits of paper around on the floor. Then without warning he let out a cry. 'Caramba!' – that's what great detectives say when they make a discovery. 'Do you see what's happened, Ignatius? Do you see what it says if we put these in a line? . . . HEAR THEM, TO READ, MARK, LEARN AND . . .'

'Well done, Sherlock!' said the mouse. 'But I still don't get it.'

'Patience, mouse,' said the furry sleuth. 'We must sleep on it.'

And sleep they did, right under the choir stalls. When morning came, they were woken by bells. 'Is it a fire?' said Sherlock, always suspicious.

'Of course not,' said the mouse. 'Today's Sunday, and the church service is about to begin. We're trapped.'

Just as he said that they saw, from underneath the seats, a procession of feet going by. First came a lot of brightly coloured

trainers. 'That's the choir,' Ignatius whispered. These were
followed by a lot of enormous muddy black boots. 'That must be
the servers,' he said. At the end there came a pair of old brown
shoes that needed a polish. 'That's the Vicar,' Ignatius said.

The service began, and they listened as the Vicar read the
special prayer for that Sunday:

'Blessed Lord, who caused all holy Scriptures to be written for
our learning: help us so to hear them, to read, mark . . .' Sherlock
and Ignatius sat bolt upright as they heard those words.

'. . . learn and inwardly digest them that, through patience,
and the comfort of your holy word, we may embrace and for ever
hold fast the blessed hope of everlasting life . . .'

The mouse and the weasel were so excited they didn't know
what to do. At last they'd discovered what all those torn bits of
paper were talking about, and Ignatius was jumping up and down
on the spot, going, 'holy scriptures! holy scriptures! holy scriptures!'

As they hid there, they could hear the Vicar telling the people
that this meant the Bible. He was saying how people should *hear*
the Bible when they come to church, and as well as this should
read it in their homes. They should *mark* it – that means
remember it – and let it really sink in, the same as you *digest* your
food. Because, he went on, if you want to be followers of Jesus,
you've got to hang on to what he teaches in the Bible – you've got
to *embrace* it and *hold fast*.

'Isn't he finished yet?' whispered Sherlock.

'Not long,' said the mouse, and as soon as the Vicar finished
speaking, they slipped out. The mystery was solved. And they
were so proud of those mysterious scraps of paper, they just
couldn't bear to eat them for their tea.

**Blessed Lord, who caused all holy Scriptures to be
written for our learning: help us so to hear them, to read,
mark, learn and inwardly digest them that, through
patience, and the comfort of your holy word, we may
embrace and for ever hold fast the hope of everlasting life,
which you have given us in our Saviour Jesus Christ.**

THE GRAND OLD MALDEN QUADRUPED'S MARATHON RACE

E veryone knew Arfa, the disgusting camel. (He got that name because when he was born they took one look at him and said, 'Yuk, this isn't 'arf a disgusting camel'). Not so many people knew his nephew, who was a giraffe. In honour of his uncle they'd called him Girarfa. Nobody liked him much, because he always looked down on other people – which giraffes tend to do.

Early one morning, as Girarfa lay happily snoring in his special giraffe's bed, with its extension for long necks, something dropped through his letterbox with a loud plonk and woke him up. So he hobbled to the door, snuffling and coughing, and picked up a long envelope with the mayor's shield stamped on the top. As quickly as his sleepy hoofs could manage, he tore it open, and found an important-looking letter headed: Grand Old Malden Quadrupeds' Marathon Race. He grunted with a puzzled grunt, because he'd never heard of a quadruped before. He got out his dictionary and looked up the word, and found that a quadruped was any animal with four legs. He looked down and started counting his legs. 'One, two, three, four – jolly good, I must be a quadruped!' he decided.

The letter went on to say that there was going to be a four-legged race, and the prize was — to be mayor for the day. 'Wonderful,' thought Girarfa, 'I've always fancied myself as a mayor.' What he really fancied was having everyone admire him and think how important he was.

At long last the day of the race arrived, and all the quadrupeds were there. Crusty old Major Feele-Gloomy felt really left out, with only two legs. So he got together with Arfa's old friend Frank, and they borrowed a pantomime suit, and went disguised as a horse.

There was one competitor that not many people knew, a quiet, furry little creature called Eric. Eric the ferret. He was the sort of animal that people didn't notice, because he kept quietly to himself.

What they all had to do was to run as fast as they could from the school down to the main road at Plough Green. Then back to the church, up to the top of the tower, down again and back to the school.

As they lined up in the playground the crowd grew silent. In the mind of Girarfa there was only one thought. At all costs he must win, by fair means or foul. He had to be mayor for the day, and have everyone admire him.

There was a loud bang, a puff of smoke, the crowd roared, and they were off.

The first thing that happened was that Major Feele-Gloomy, who was the front legs of the horse, kept stamping with his great, black, shiny, military boots on the feet of poor Frank, who was the back legs. So over they tumbled, and every time they tried to get up, over they went again. That's what you get for pretending to be a quadruped.

As for the rest, it was neck and neck round the corner and along Church Road. Arfa the camel hadn't run anywhere for years, he was so disgustingly lazy. As soon as he reached the library he was so puffed out he collapsed on the bench, wheezing horribly, and try as he might, he just couldn't get up again. The rest of them raced on down to the main road, with Ignatius the church mouse in the lead. Suddenly he saw a steam-roller heading straight for him. What could he do? Quick as a flash, the nimble mouse jumped on a passing bus, and the next thing he knew – he was in Kingston. So Harold the Mole was the first to get to Plough Green. But he was so daft, and so gormless, that once he got there he forgot what to do next, so he burrowed under the earth.

That left just two of them racing back to the church, Girarfa and Eric the ferret. Girarfa tried every trick he could think of. He tried to barge Eric into the pond with a swing of his long neck. He tried to trip him up with his bony great shin. He even threw down banana skins left over from his breakfast. But Eric just kept going.

When they reached the church, Girarfa charged up the tower, shoving Eric to one side. But the ladders in the tower, sad to say, weren't all that safe. Just as Girarfa was getting near the top, he trod on a rotten step and with a mighty crash fell through.

'Help me, Eric,' he whimpered feebly, as he hung by his hoof tips over the great drop. 'I didn't mean to play all those tricks on